NOON

Editor	DIANE WILLIAMS
Senior Editor	CHRISTINE SCHUTT
Associate Editor	LAURA KIRK
Editorial Staff	DOROTHEA CHERINGTON
	REBECCA GODFREY
	JACOB WILLIAMS
Managing Editor	MATT MAYERCHAK
Development Associate	RICK WHITAKER
Copyeditor	RICHARD G. GALLIN
Directors	BILL HAYWARD
	CHRISTINE SCHUTT
	DAVID SLATER
	KATHRYN STALEY
	HAMZA WALKER
	DIANE WILLIAMS

NOON is an independent not-for-profit literary annual published by NOON, Inc.

Edition price $9.00 (domestic) or $14.00 (foreign)
All donations are tax deductible.

—

NOON is distributed by
Ingram Periodicals, Inc., 18 Ingram Boulevard,
La Vergne, Tennessee 37086 (800) 627-6247 and

SPD/Small Press Distribution, Inc.
1341 Seventh Street, Berkeley, CA 94710
(510) 524-1668 • www.spdbooks.org

Bernhard DeBoer, Inc., 113 East Centre Street,
Nutley, New Jersey 07110 (973) 667-9300

NOON welcomes submissions. Send to:
Diane Williams
NOON 1369 Madison Avenue PMB 298 New York New York 10128
Please include the necessary self-addressed, stamped envelope.

ISSN 1526-8055
ISBN 0-9676211-6-X
© 2006 by NOON, Inc.
All rights reserved *Printed in U.S.A.*

NOON is indexed by *The American Humanities Index.*

Cover art: *Oote Boe/PictureArts*

CONTENTS

The Editors proudly congratulate Rebecca Curtis,
recipient of a 2005 Rona Jaffe Foundation Writer's Award.

SOMEONE LIKE SUE

REBECCA CURTIS

Recently my husband and I came into a large sum of money. The way we came into it was, we found it lying on the sidewalk in the form of someone's wallet. We also found one diamond earring nearby and a wad of cash. We took it all right home. But after touching everything for a while, we put it down on the table and called the paper to place an ad asking if anyone had lost a wallet, an earring, and a cash wad. We hoped no one would answer, but we wanted to do things the way the regulations required.

Soon enough there was a call. When I really thought about it, I knew there'd be a call. The woman on the phone called herself "Amy," and she spoke in a teeny, tiny voice, but I knew she was really Sue, my friend from college, and I knew she'd probably spent the whole morning reading the paper looking for ads that asked people if they'd lost any money. That was the kind of thing Sue would do. It was probably how she was getting by. My husband and I are honest people and we both work horrible teaching jobs and we live in an apartment that smells like sauerkraut and has only two windows, both of which look on to the interstate, so I resent people like Sue.

Hello, I said, what's your name?

I'm Amy, the woman said. Amy.

All right, I said. I was already disgusted. Well, I said, I need to ask you some questions the regulations require me to ask. I sat down at the table in front of a yellow legal pad, the kind my husband likes and keeps hundreds of around to take notes on.

All right, she said.

Where do you live? I said.

New York City, she said. It was nowhere near where we'd found the money.

Who is your health insurance with? I said.

There was a pause. Silver Castle, she said.

Fine, I said. I wrote it down, "Silver Castle," a respected name in health insurance.

Wait, she said. I don't really have health insurance.

You don't? I said. I was surprised that she'd lied so soon, but I wasn't surprised that she didn't have health insurance. She'd had a lot of problems in college, and she'd almost dropped out at one point. I crossed out "Silver Castle health insurance."

I have called them several times though, she said, to ask health-related questions, and they've been answering me, and they've given me advice. So I guess in a way I do have Silver Castle health insurance.

Oh, I said.

The man I spoke with was Richard Walton, she said, and he's in claims and appeals.

Her answer seemed official, so I wrote down, "Richard Walton, Silver Castle health insurance." I knew I could check on it by calling up Silver Castle and asking for him, but I also knew I'd probably never do it.

Well, I said. I guess I asked you the questions. I'll call you when we've submitted the answers and gotten the results.

You still need to ask me how old I am, she said.

She was right. There were several questions I hadn't bothered with because I knew it was Sue on the phone.

How old? I said.

Twenty-nine, she said.

That was Sue's age. I wrote it down.

What do you do? I said.

I buy a lot of makeup and jewelry, she said.

I wrote down, "Buys makeup and jewelry."

Do you get paid for that? I said.

No, she said. I don't. Right now I don't really have a job.

Fine, I said. Good-bye, Sue. Then I hung up.

I sat down on the couch. My husband sat down next to me. The couch smelled, because of all the food crumbs he'd dropped in its cracks, because he eats on the couch and is clumsy. The smell made me hate him a bit, along with the fact that the couch had cracks, but he was acting husbandly and touching my hair. He wanted to know what I was thinking and what Sue had said on the phone. This is what I was thinking:

The fact that Sue didn't have a job didn't surprise me. The last I knew, after college, she'd been working at a large department store. But I always thought she'd lose the job, especially because she was so small — she only weighed ninety pounds and she was only five feet tall. Her smallness seemed to point to something about her everyone could see, that she was untrustworthy and could be easily beaten up. Not many people had trusted her in college, and a lot of people had beaten her up. She had a knack for getting into bad relationships — she'd dated a rapist, a wife beater, a narcissistic guitar player, and another rapist, in that order. Both rapists raped her, the wife beater beat her, and the guitar player wrote her a lot of narcissistic love poems before leaving her for a big blonde debutante who walked like a duck. The rapists didn't exactly leave her — one of them raped her for quite a while. With the wife beater, the relationship just kind of fell apart. She wanted to get married and he didn't, was the problem. Of course, I tried to be a good friend through all this. For starters, I loaned her money. She wasn't good with money, and although we were only in college, she already had several credit cards. Afterward, she never paid me back, although she claimed she had — she claimed she'd put the money in my mailbox one day, but it was never there. I looked many times. When I told her the money wasn't there, she said someone had probably seen the money and taken it out, which made sense since the mailboxes had no doors. I didn't believe her, but I still tried to be her good friend. I ate in the dining hall with her, and I nodded my head when she said that one day she planned to go to the gym and work out. I went to parties with her so she could meet up with the men who raped her, and after she met up with them I wandered around by myself, looking for someone to have my own bad relationship with, until eventually I gave up and went home. Neither one of us knew why she kept dating the men who raped her, except that they were handsome and she had fun with them sometimes. She never had fun with me because I was a big drip at that time. But in the afternoons, after she'd been raped, I would always listen to her cry and comb her hair while she sat in awkward, painful positions on the floor, and I always repressed the urge to rape her myself. She had long black hair, a tiny body as I've said, a heart-shaped face, and beautiful little brown legs like a table in the Rococo style. I knew our friendship wasn't healthy for me, because she often hurt my feelings by telling me I looked fat from the front but not from the side and that I should stand sideways most of the time. She also said I was depressing, which was why I didn't have any friends. But her friendship brought me a lot of benefits, like the way we held hands when we entered a party, and how all the guys thought that looked good, and when I thought about the money I'd loaned her that she never paid back, I knew that in a way she thought I owed her the money, because of all those times we'd held hands.

My husband touched my hair. Then he asked me who'd called, and I explained that it was Sue, my friend from college, but that she was calling herself Amy now and didn't have a job. I told him she'd been looking through the paper and seen our ad and called.

Don't give her the money, he said. Promise you won't.

He said that because I'm soft at heart.

All right, I said. But I knew I would.

She called again the next day, to ask who else had called to claim the money, and I admitted no one had.

I tried to ask her some trick questions, but she gave good answers right away.

How much money? I said. How much money in the wad?

A lot, she said. All I had.

What did the diamond earring look like?

Like glass, she said. But not.

That's right, I said, so far, but whose name was on the credit cards in the wallet? I was sure I had her there.

Look, she said. She paused. I can't tell you the name on the credit cards. I use fake names sometimes and I can't repeat them on the phone. But it's mine. You've got to believe me. I answered all the other questions right. And I need the money. I don't make much money buying jewelry.

I thought you didn't get paid, I said.

I don't, she said. I buy the jewelry and wear it and then I bring it back the next week. I always shop at different stores.

I could see my husband making violent motions in the kitchen. Then he held up a head of lettuce to indicate how much we needed money ourselves.

I'm trying to be fair, I said to Sue, but we both know the money is better off with me.

That may be true, she said, but it's my money, and I need it more.

I thought about when my husband and I found the money. Sue was nowhere in sight. But she could have been down any alley, beaten to a pulp, and even though I hadn't done it to her, I had done it to her in my head many times.

I saw my husband watching from the kitchen.

Don't you give her the money, he said.

Let me ask you one last question, I said, and if you answer right, I'll give you the money.

Go, she said.

Tell me truly, I said: Are you really Sue?

No, she said, I'm Amy. She used her teeny fake voice to say this.

No, I said, you're not.

I'm Amy.

You're Sue.

If I say I'm Sue, she said in a teeny voice, will you give me the money?

Yes, I said.

I'm Sue! she said. Her teeny fake voice fell away. I was Sue all this time, she screamed, in her more regular voice. Ha ha ha!

I knew I'd lost. I told her to tell me her address and she did and I wrote it down. I am a woman of my word. I could see my husband despairing in the kitchen, holding up piles of unpaid bills. He was a good man, a loser who loved me and was saddled with loans. How could I explain to him? The truth was, I could not.

I could never explain to him, because he would never understand the attraction in someone like Sue, how she could wrap her teeny tiny self around your heart and squeeze it until you were purple.

HE LIVED ON LOVER'S PEAK

ROB WALSH

The ingredients were men and wood. That's how you build a house. It was going to stand while people died in it, and then some more died, and finally one other, who left behind a legal statement. That statement commanded his possessions go to the least of all relatives, the relative who knew dirt, the relative who lived way down underneath everybody else.

This is the story of the relative who lived way down underneath everybody else. It tells how he got a house and paintings of ruddy sailboats and boxes stacked against the wall.

But the first thing he got was a bank account. Before this, all he had was a full beard.

He lived on Lover's Peak. That's where his house was. When

the parked teenagers saw him gardening in the dirt they jacked their eyes up. Eventually he went inside to eat some fruit salad.

His mother worked for an assembly line and had just become forty. She reached out and felt his beard.

"If you cut it, life will be good to you. It will recognize you again."

His mother was something of an angel. She knew how to walk into a room and make it smell spicy. He decided to take a job at the assembly line and figure her out.

On his first day when his mother took a break, she asked if he'd like anything from the bakery.

"I'd like some fruit salad," he said.

"What about to drink?" his mother asked.

"Milk would be nice," he said.

While she was away, a miter saw and a rotating power press malfunctioned and cut the man's hand off.

From then on the man stayed close to his house on Lover's Peak.

Outside, the teenagers were at it. One squirmed like an octopus. She punched with her torso. The man tried to make sense of it. His erection was going to stand independently in the background.

DOG AND ME

LYDIA DAVIS

An ant can look up at you, too, and even threaten you with its arms. Of course, my dog does not know I am human. He sees me as dog, though I do not leap up at a fence. I am a strong dog. But I do not leave my mouth hanging open when I walk along. Even on a hot day, I do not leave my tongue hanging out. But I bark at him: "No! No!"

GETTING TO KNOW
YOUR BODY

LYDIA DAVIS

If your eyeballs move, this means that you're thinking, or about to start thinking.

If you don't want to be thinking at this particular moment, try to keep your eyeballs still.

THE CATERPILLAR

LYDIA DAVIS

I find a small caterpillar in my bed in the morning. There is no good window to throw him from and I don't crush or kill a living thing if I don't have to. I will go to the trouble of carrying this thin, dark, hairless little caterpillar down the stairs and out to the garden. It is not an inchworm, though it is the size of an inchworm. It does not hump up in the middle but travels steadily along on its many pairs of legs. As I leave the bedroom, it is quite speedily walking around the slopes of my hand. But halfway down the stairs, it is gone — my hand is blank on every side. The caterpillar must have let go and dropped. I can't see him. The stairwell is dim, and the stairs are painted dark brown. I could get a flashlight and search for this tiny thing, in order to save his life. But I will not go that far — he will have to do the best he can. Yet how could he make his way down to the back door and out into the garden? I go on about my business. I think I've forgotten him, but I haven't. Every time I go upstairs or down, I am avoiding his side of the stairs. I am sure he is there trying to get down. At last I give in. I get the flashlight. Now the trouble is that the stairs are so dirty. I don't clean them because no one ever sees them here in the dark. And the caterpillar is, or was, so small. Many things under the beam of the flashlight look somewhat like him — a very slim splinter of wood or a thick piece of thread. But when I poke them, they don't move. I look on every step on his side of the stairs, and then on both sides. You get somewhat attached to any living thing once you try to help it. But he is nowhere. There is so much dust and dog hair on the steps. The dust may have stuck to his little body and made it hard for him to move or at least to go in the direction he wanted to go in. It may have dried him out. But why would he even go down instead of up? I haven't looked on the landing above where he disappeared. I will not go that far. I go back to my work. Then I begin to forget the caterpillar. I forget him for as long as one hour, until I happen to go to the stairs again. The next time I think of him, I see that I have forgotten him for several hours. I think of him when I go up or down the stairs. After all, he is really there somewhere, trying to find his way to a green leaf, or dying. But already I don't care as much. My attachment to him was slight, and didn't last long. When I leave the stairs I forget him again. Soon, I'm sure, I will forget him entirely. Now I see that there is something just the right size, shape, and color on one of the steps, but it is so flat and dry I think it can't have started out as him. It is a short pine needle or some other plant part. Later there is an unpleasant animal smell lingering about the stairwell, but he is too small to have any smell. He has probably died. He is too small for me to continue thinking about him. I'm sure I will not think about him again, after today.

ABSENTMINDED

LYDIA DAVIS

The cat is crying at the window. It wants to come in. You think about how living with a cat and the demands of a cat make you think about simple things, like a cat's need to come indoors, and how good that is. You think about this, and you are too busy thinking about this to let the cat in, so you forget to let the cat in, and it is still at the window crying. You see that you haven't let the cat in, and you think about how odd it is that while you were thinking about the cat's needs and how good it is to live with the simple needs of a cat you were not letting the cat in but letting it go on crying at the window. Then while you're thinking about this and how odd it is, you let the cat in without knowing you're letting the cat in. Now the cat jumps up onto the washing machine and cries for food. You see that the cat is crying for food, but you don't think of feeding it because you are thinking how odd it is that you have let the cat in without knowing it. Then you see that it's crying for food while you're not feeding it, and as you see this and think it's odd that you have not heard it cry, you feed the cat without knowing that you're feeding it.

PHOTOGRAPHS

BILL HAYWARD

These collaborative portraits — produced at more than thirty historic sites across the nation — begin with this understood provocation: Deliver yourself! All the words, marks, cut paper, and constructions are created by the subjects. Bill Hayward's *The American Memory Project* — inaugurated in 2002 — is a work in progress, producing historic markers for the twenty-first century. As of today, two hundred citizens are participants.

SCOTT B. SMITH, JR.

Civil Rights Activist, 1965 Bloody Sunday Voting Rights March

Selma, Alabama

AMANDA ROTH

Student

Lafayette College

Easton, Pennsylvania

DANA

Eighth-grade student

Craryville, New York

I'M HAVING A
NORMAL DAY
I'M INNOCENT UNTIL
PROVEN GUILTY
I didn't smile
all DAY

ADAM HAZLETT

Photographer

Dealey Plaza

Dallas, Texas

CATHY BARNER

Director, Parks Projects

Golden Gate National Parks Conservancy

San Francisco, California

AL PACILE

Environmentalist

Cerillos, New Mexico

DONNA CARNEY

Artist

Easton, Pennsylvania

WALLACE COFFEY

Cultural Resources Specialist

Institute of American Indian Arts

Santa Fe, New Mexico

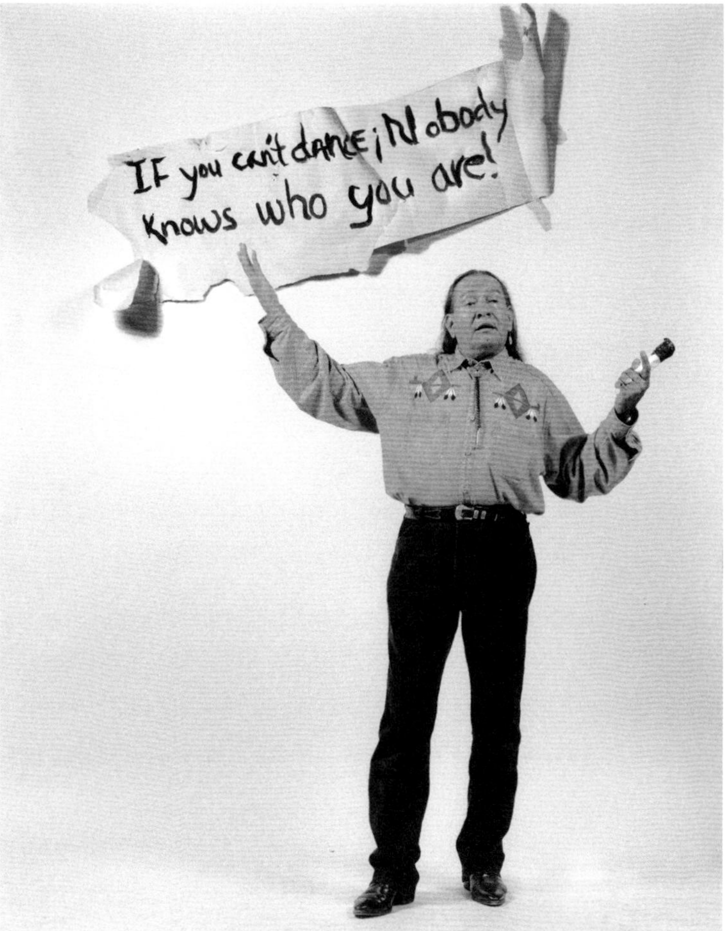
If you can't dance ¡Nobody knows who you are!

THE DUCHESS OF ALBANY

CHRISTINE SCHUTT

"The garden dies with the gardener" was what Owen had said, but when, years later, he died, she faced the garden with a will to keep it alive — as who would not? But the twins urged her to sell. They thought it would be wise to move out of the house (for too long too large) and into Wax Hill with its assisted-care conveniences and attached hospital: Wax Hill that short line to the furnace and the thoroughfare.

She had carried Owen's chalky bones in a bag. She had tossed him into every part of the garden. How could she sell the house when from every window in the house — and there were lots of windows — she could see some part of him, Owen, her well-named spirit with meaty gardener's hands and other contradictions. He liked the slow and melancholy; he listened to *St. Matthew's Passion* long after Easter. But God? He didn't believe. Young once, he saw himself alone when he was old with just a daughter. He left behind two, not of his own making but full of reverence for him, nonetheless.

He was a schoolteacher, and the luggage-colored oak leaves signaled his season, but it had come around so fast. He had had nuns for cousins—nuns! Sisters of Charity, how queer they seemed now; their menace, vanished. Mustachioed Agnes Gertrude and arthritic Mary Agnes, they had taught at the Mount for forty-odd years, wimpled and sudden, full of authority.

She said, "I haven't seen a nun in such a long, long time."

The twins, on conference call, were hard to tell apart except when they laughed.

She didn't have a lot to say and lapsed into what the weather was doing. Today snow, the second snowstorm of the new year—and Owen once in it. She could see him, lopsided, clowny, a scarf around his head. Blizzardy weather was wonderful to walk in.

"Oh, Mother," from the twins when she cried. Overly dramatic, yes, she knew she was being, but she missed him. The wide road he had offered her each morning, saying, "What's on your agenda?" Now the wide road had all the charm of a freeway.

"But take a walk," the twins said, "if it's snowing."

Inward would be a nice word for what she was, *self-absorbed* would be more accurate.

"I know the country is at war," she said; nevertheless, she

missed him. "Besides, when I look at the larger world, I cry almost as much."

But there was Owen, his voice, the sound of him in another room, off-key hummer, cracking nuts over the paper, singing or whistling a patter song. A Gilbert and Sullivan tune twiddled for days: "The lady novelist . . . I'm sure she'd not be missed." Whatever he thought to play or heard was his favorite. "I've got a little list . . . I'm sure she'd not be missed."

Some nights now she plunged into working, but vodka some mornings was preferred. She had to admit it—to herself but not to the twins.

She told them, "I have started a sestina." She said she was inspired by Elizabeth Bishop's "Sestina," and she was using two of the same words. "The line, *Time to plant tears*, was what moved me."

"Sestinas are difficult," the twins said. Her educated daughters, they knew, they had tried. "In high school, Mother. Remember Miss Byrd?"

"Oh, Miss Byrd!" and they had a rare good laugh, the three of them, she and the twins, remembering the ethereal Miss Byrd, giddy and overworked and walking into walls. The twins laughed about Miss Byrd getting lost in the mall on the Boston trip. The twins were laughing, and she was laughing a little, too, when the sight of the old dog asleep alarmed her. And on a sudden, in the whiplash moodiness of youth, she was mad at Owen. Damn him. "There's no pleasure to be had in discipline and restraint," she said to the twins. "That's what a fucking sestina is all about," and so the pleasure of laughing was over.

"Why, Mother?" One voice.

The other said, "You've been drinking."

She said, "I don't have to defend myself." Besides, she explained, the drinking was only a problem if she drove, "and I don't." She stayed at the table or slept in the big chair and no one need worry. She might die there — no mess.

"Mother!"

"All I am saying is you can't have much of an accident if you sit somewhere with a drink."

"You have to get up for the bottle." Only Clarissa would say. Here was the difference between her girls: one was meaner than the other.

"I bring the bottle to the table."

"Great, Mother. That's just great. Now do you see why we don't want to call?"

"Then don't. Leave me alone." And she hung up the phone and almost kicked at the dog, but she refrained. The dog was her friend. Pink. "Poor, old Pink," she said, "you scared the shit out of me," and she leaned out to pat a shapeless pile of fuzz and spoke nonsense to it, Owen's dog, Pink, adopted, a miniature mix of something abandoned and abused. Pink was hairless at the start. "Look at you now, you little dust cloth, baby Pink, old sweetie. I wouldn't hurt you. You're my pal."

"I'm on the move today," she said to Pink, but the dog lay unperturbed, sure she would come back.

· · ·

A snowstorm, a thaw, a brilliant sun, snow, freezing temperatures, snow, then better, warmer, promising weather arrived, and she looked back at Pink and then to the rake and the garden where the wet, mahogany islands of leaves, submerged for months in snow, now floated. All the snow pelted away by a rain the night before and only a mist this morning, something more than fog. She liked to work in it. She thought of Owen's hair — water-beaded and in the sun brightly netted. She raked and thought if the twins could see. If they could live with the garden the way she did. Covered or uncovered, leafed or bare, the garden was restorative in any season. The persistent mist was turning into rain. March, late March. Somebody's birthday — whose?

She abandoned Pink to the mud. She raked the beds; she swept the pavers. "Dirty girl!" she said when the dog wobbled toward her. Why had she even taken the poor mutt out? The dog trembled and squeaked.

The six words in her sestina are *garden*, *widow*, *husband*, *dog*, *almanac*, *tears*. "The envoy is an oncoming train." She said, "Restrain the wild element of mourning and what you get is sentimentality."

The twins, she should listen to them, sell, move, secure what there was to secure for them. Poor girls, in the disarray of single life, the yap, yap, yap of the dryer at the Laundromat beating up their tired clothes. Few single men where they lived, and the best of them gay.

The rain was cold, but she let herself get wet the way Owen did until she was soaked.

In the kitchen again she lit up the stove and watched the rain wash the garden into its outline. Green spikes stippled the beds she had raked, and the cropped crowns of established plants, the wheat-colored stalks of hydrangea, poked out polished in a design of circles mostly.

If her daughters could only see.

How is it possible that in caring for the garden she could miss summer? How is it possible, but she did.

Up at four and again at five, and at five-thirty up for good. Pink was awake; she heard him tick against the bare floor, circling the bed; she heard him yawn. "Good morning," she said, and she went on talking to Pink as she carried the dog down the stairs and to the paper. "Because it's too cold outside, isn't it, Pinkie? I'm not going to do what I did yesterday. Too cold and wet this morning." She saw forty-five on the thermometer. The radio said it was colder. Too cold. She got water, aspirin, more water. She put on deodorant, then went back to bed. For how long? Who cared? She was up again besides. She washed her hair and dried it in the heat of the open oven.

Once she had thought it would be hard to let go of life, but it will not be so hard.

She read; she wrote; she must have had lunch but she could not remember. The scenes that blew past came out in bands of color. The wispy complication of bare branches was added magic; the shadows were dark and sure. She put Owen in her poem, Owen or the shape of him, on the deck in his coat and pompomed hat, a passenger on a steamer, a blanket over his legs, heavy sweater, scarf — the pom-pomed hat. The garden beyond him she turned into straw.

Why did she lie to the twins? Why, when they called, did she say, "I am not drinking. I am working." Why didn't she tell them, "I'm doing both"?

The brief hello of summer and its long, long good-bye. Great piles of death she hauled to the woods to the dead pile. Farewell to the flowers of summer, to plume poppy and *Vernonia*. Turk's-cap lilies, delicate as paper lanterns at the height of their glowing, good-bye.

"Anytime you care to look," Owen said whenever he caught her watching his quick strip at the back door. She liked to look at his secreted machinery from behind when he bent over or stood one-legged getting out of his shorts. There it was, the long, dark purse of him asway. The head of his cock was the color of putty. Its expression was aloof most of the time, a self-satisfied indifference. When he was seated in some other ablution, the head of his cock was rosy and large and also arousing.

All she ever had to do was ask when what she liked to do most was look. Look!

"It's yours," he said, and with a flourish held out the bouquet of himself, "be my guest."

. . .

Overnight, age seemed to happen to him, then a few years of *ifs*, poorer health, and medication.

"Don't talk of moving just yet, please," she told the twins. "Not tonight."

Why, except for loneliness, did she answer the phone? (Owen at the long table, saying to the ringing phone, "Go away people. Leave us alone," and people pretty much did.) To get off the phone she used the excuse of Pink somewhere sick. The odd thing was when she did hang up, she found Pink in the closet sick.

"Poor baby," she said.

"Old age," said the vet.

He gave Pink pills that worked to ward off motion sickness, which sometimes happened to old pets, despite their stationary lives. "He will sleep a little bit more."

"A good night's sleep," she said. "Wouldn't that be nice?"

They talked a little, she and the old vet, for he, too, was old. They talked about Owen, or she did, and he asked, "Have you looked for any groups?" On the swizzling drive home in the rain, she cried, and she couldn't see to drive and had to pull over. "Fucking old vet!" She put her face in her hands and cried. She petted Pink and cooed at him a little, saying, "We won't go back there again, will we, Pinkie. No, no. But you feel better already, don't you." The little dog was a dust ball; just petting him made her feel awful. "Do I have to outlive everybody?"

"Yes, yes, yes, no," she said. "The lily-of-the-valley is up." She said, "Yes, it was two years ago today."

"We wanted you to know, we're thinking about you," the twins said, and the girls called again later just to see how she was. "How are you, Mommy?" they asked in maternal voices.

"The lily-of-the-valley is up," she said.

May was his birthday month and hers, when she and Owen quietly celebrated with nothing more than mild surprise. He was given to saying, "I think I'm going to see another spring." And he did — just.

Heart.

Of course, his heart, what else?

Now the oppressive immovable quality of objects wore her out.

"Mother!"

Whatever was not in front of her she meant to remember. His shapely head, his small red ear, his hair.

"You've been drinking. We can tell."

"We knew you would."

"So why act so surprised?" She hung up the phone and saw the fucking dog peeing on the floor in front of her. Little fucker!

They had not had enough time, she and Owen.

· · ·

"I'm no such thing," she said to the twins.

Another night, "I'm tired."

Another, "I'm old is what it is."

Owen had said that in the garden she would rediscover childhood, but those childhood experiences she remembered were mostly dreadful. She took her nose out of the flower, and her cousin, seeing her, laughed. "Your nose!" The red was hard to get off as were grass stains on her knees and elbows. Childhood in the garden. The garden was not genteel. The garden was full of thugs, and Owen had shown her some. The 'Duchess of Albany' was not a thug, but a racer on a brittle stem, a *Clematis* with deep pink upside down bells, deceptively frail and well-bred, small, timorous bells. The 'Duchess of Albany' was a favorite of hers: how could she sell the house to someone who might kill the Duchess in the earth-moving business of house improvement.

"The men came, yes," she said to her daughters. "But they have such big feet!" she said. "They can't help it, I know."

"Mommy!" the twins said. "We're only trying to help."

So was she. Hadn't she consented to the ugly tub? That ugly tub with the gruff bottom and the grips.

Her children have not visited in years.

"Oh, Mother," they say, "what are you talking about?"

49.

. . .

She took her own safety precautions and moved her bedroom, such as it was, downstairs to the sun porch. On the sun porch on the sofa she was not afraid to fall asleep.

What made Pink nest in corners? "What do you think is the matter?" she asked.

"Pink's old, Mommy."

"The dog's ancient. Take him to the vet's."

"Oh, god," she said. Going to the old vet's frightened her as much as it did the dog. "Oh, god," she said. She felt so bogged down and muddled.

"You're drunk is what you are": from the meaner?

"Oh, god," she said. "I don't want to find a stiff dog under the desk. I don't, I don't, I don't." She cried and the twins consoled her.

"Mommy, why don't you crawl into your cream puff and go to sleep for a while?"

"You and the dog have a snooze."

She said, "I think I will." She said, "Pink doesn't realize I have mixed feelings about him."

She had found him in an odd posture tipped against the shed. The hose was squiggled over half the garden, and elsewhere were two full buckets, a shovel, a rake. How she had wished, for his sake, Owen had put away the tools and coiled the hose and achieved a perfect death, although the twins yelled at her for saying such a thing.

But the morning after he died, the terrible morning after, repeats so many times a day: she woke up, dressed, walked downstairs, made her gritty breakfast drink, and took her tea outside. Then she saw it, the grain bin, where he kept his garden clothes and she fell to her knees and cried. Up to that moment, she had sipped at her tea and believed he was alive and already in the garden and muddy.

The permanence of his absence is a noise she hears when she listens to how quiet. How he did and he did and he did for her.

"Can I be of any help?" Always he asked this, "Do you want anything? Can I get you anything?"

She thought it was summer still if not spring, but the day's evidence said it was fall. Again!

"When was the last time you were outside, Mommy?"

"I'm taking care of the garden." She told them her nose was in it, brushing against the staining anthers, freakishly marked, a bald animal, she, a stiff, kinked dog, not unlike the dog she owned. Pink. Pink, what was the matter with that dog? After she got off the phone, she caught him in the act and pulled him away, made him stop, put him out of doors — like that — then wiped up after him. She brought Pink inside and carried Pink to his bed in the kitchen and talked to him. But even as she apologized for the choke hold, a part of her wished him dead and another part feared his dying, and she took Pink upstairs and bathed him in the new tub. His pink skin was so pink he looked scalded. He was thin;

he shivered, though she was gentle and the water was warm. She dried him with her own soft towel and when he was dried and happy and at ease, she swaddled and rocked him. He was so pitifully thin. She put him in his cream puff and said, "I'm getting into mine."

I WAS SUPPOSED TO END

KIM CHINQUEE

I was supposed to end at 3:15, but I had nothing else to say. So I ended class early. I'd been sitting in my office, watching the dead leaves that hung on to the ground. My students had written poems that day about getting out of handcuffs. One student wrote a poem about his hard-on, and the other one, a poem to me, about how he thought he'd disappointed me — he'd wondered if that was why I'd canceled several classes, and changed my style of teaching. I had worn a thin gown that exposed my lower body.

I heard the ringing of my cell phone; it was my son.

I addressed him as a pronoun.

THIS ONE

KIM CHINQUEE

He said to boil an egg. He was at the gym, and she had finished running.

First she boiled water, but when she dropped the egg in, the shell cracked and the white stuff started bubbling. So she started over with a new egg, this time warming both together. After a couple minutes, she checked the egg, cutting it, but it wasn't done yet. So she tried another, leaving it while she took a shower.

Naked, she threw away the eggs she'd spoiled, and peeled the shell off this hopeful one.

CLEAN CUT

KIM CHINQUEE

One had known me forever. The other was new, clean-cut, plaid cotton. The old one had dark hair and T-shirts. I chose the new one. I don't know why. I had some papers making me important. They wanted me for my papers. I felt sorry for the old one, his dripping head. I drifted back. Then the new one gave me money. I needed relief. I had nothing of my own besides those papers. The old one wanted to talk. We rode in his polka-dotted car. He said please marry me, and I said I'm with the other. He had a gun. It wasn't my fault. The bullet went through his arm. I went back to the new one, pure as a newborn. The old one said sorry for that bullet, and could he cut my hair. I was getting ready for a great night with the new one. I looked at myself. He, the old one, had shaved a side of my head, and left a clean cut. He pointed to his head, and he said, "See?" He had something just like it. I remembered he'd always had that. I don't know why.

HEIFER

KIM CHINQUEE

I was in my shorts and halter top with my Holstein, Tootles. My father gave her to me right after she was born. On her certificate, I was listed as the owner.

The breeder had put a seed inside her. I liked the breeder's son — he left notes in my desk along with squares of Hubba Bubba. In our notes, we debated names for Tootles' offspring. We came up with Twinkles, Twix, and Tootsie.

I'd tied her to a pole. I was brushing her. She'd be going to the fair, where I would lead her in a coliseum, and a judge would evaluate her legs and spine and posture, and she'd get a blueredwhitepink ribbon, all depending. Last year she got a red for body structure, but a pink for showmanship, which was mostly my fault.

She grunted. "It's okay," I said. I saw a hint of red coming from her muzzle.

My grandfather worked for the Grain Elevator, and I saw him coming over, still in his dusty overalls. His legs moved, each like a separate caterpillar, inching. He was tall, and he reminded me of Slinky.

He used to live in the house where I was living. He used to have my bedroom. He had owned it. Now my grandpa lived in a trailer with his wife in a small town called Pulaski.

"Hi, Grandpa Jeans," I said. He sat on a gigantic stone behind me.

He asked me where my dad was. He was hay baling with my mother. I told my grandfather I didn't know where my dad was.

"Where's Bethie?" he said. My younger twin.

"A 4-H thing," I said. We were the You-Better-Get-Em Getters.

He found a brush and started on Tootles. I told him that I thought she had a nosebleed. He told me it was nothing. He brushed her hard and fierce-like. She grunted. I saw red coming from her muzzle. "It's fine," I said.

I SCOOPED VANILLA
BY THE DOZENS

KIM CHINQUEE

I scooped vanilla by the dozens. My biceps learned to thicken. I got used to the humming of the freezers, making clown cones to appetize the children. I was allowed one free scoop each shift, compliments of Mr. Williams, the fat man with whom I learned to be respectful. At the front, I'd cursed him. My aunts and uncles and grandparents were fat, too. When customers came in and asked for scoops, they'd ask me how I could work at an ice-cream shop and be so thin?

I wasn't fucking skinny.

One day, when my dad came in and asked for chocolate, I scooped for him. I didn't ask why he was there or anything, because that seemed more strange than not asking anything at all. So after he presented me his money, and with the birthday card he'd sent to me that got returned to him, saying it was the wrong address, asking me what happened, I said I didn't know. "Sorry, Dad," I said. "Maybe Mom gave you a different address."

He threw his cone at me. I was prepared for the unexpected. I ran to the back. I guessed Mr. Williams told my dad he had to leave. I guess it was the thing that I expected. Mr. Williams said that if I wanted, I could go somewhere better, maybe home.

I walked the path I'd walked the night before. I waited for midnight.

PHOTOGRAPHS

NEAL RANTOUL

MANAGING

DEB OLIN UNFERTH

The building manager and I shared a wall, a long wall, and this is an intimate thing. We knew each other's music and bathroom habits and could discuss them. We knew other things about each other, too, that we didn't discuss, or shall I say that she probably knew and I didn't want to admit, or shall I say I felt certain that she knew that I . . .

Things we did discuss: her one friend in the world. This was not me. This was a woman who lived fifty miles away and to whom she talked on the phone every day for hours. When the friend called I had to leave. She never went to see the friend because she wouldn't leave her apartment and the friend never came to see her because she wouldn't ride in a motor vehicle.

I knew about the car accident but I never knew why the building manager and her apartment, why that.

One day the building manager got a prank call. She told me about it over an egg. She said, Have you ever tried phone sex? Because that is what I did when he called, she said. Phone sex.

No, I said because I had not.

The next time I dropped by she said, Well, I'm expecting a phone call at seven so you'll have to leave a bit before. Then she said, Remember I told you about the phone sex guy?

I was planning to leave the area soon and forever and a certain man was involved who I planned to leave, too. I didn't see him anymore but he was there, a few blocks away in a house on the park. All right, I did still see him, late at night or early in the morning and no one knew. I couldn't face my friends anymore. It had been months and months and months and all I had done was move closer, not further.

The building was a crumbling Victorian mansion that had been split into four moldy apartments. I suppose that means the building manager was a mansion manager. The woman who lived in the basement had seven dogs, all deformed. Each one had been rescued from certain annihilation at the last possible moment. One dog had no back legs and dragged itself around on its butt. Another was covered with spongy sores. The woman from the basement walked them on seven leashes and stood in the yard with all those dogs twisting around her like White and the seven sins. The one time she spoke to me she said, That music you were playing last night — were you playing it to make fun of me?

The mansion manager said, Remember the phone sex guy?

Is he still calling?

Yes. A friend of his called the other day, too.

So now she was doing it with both of them.

Then the manager's one friend in the world was having a party. She told me about it to tell me she had decided not to go. As if she had been considering it. I think I'll skip this one, she said with a yawn.

I said to her, I'll drive you. I'll bring you to your friend.

I couldn't do that, she said. Who would take care of Sugar?

Sugar was her dog and a damn issue. The manager didn't like to leave him alone, even for a few hours. The manager had an elaborate plan about how she and Sugar would meet up, afterward. In case in the end it turned out we're just dirt and ash, she had a will signed by a lawyer that explained in detail how they would be cremated, first the dog, then her, how their ashes would be mixed, and she had a map showing where they'd be tossed. Someone would do this for them. And in case it turned out reincarnation was right, she had a plan for that, too, about how she would find Sugar if he came back reincarnated in another body, about a bandanna of a certain rare color and they would wander the earth and how this bandanna would be a sign. Somehow it was going to work out, no matter what the truth was or who had it — except the Christians, she knew that couldn't be right, but other than that, she'd have her bases covered and I have to say I thought this to be the most sensible thing about her when I think of all the maneuvers people go through not to be alone.

Did I mention the manager's one friend in the world was a chef? Yes, she was and the mansion manager listed for me all the food she was to have at the party. The deviled eggs, the potato salad, the vegetable fried rice, the Caesar salad.

You must go, I said. How can you miss it? How can you miss the Caesar salad? I knew the mansion manager had her groceries delivered. I had seen a boy come up the yard.

I'll drive you, I said. Think what it would mean to have you there.

I can't possibly go, she said. Sugar.

I'll take care of Sugar.

We looked at each other for a moment because how was I supposed to take care of Sugar if I was driving her back and forth. Then I said, Here's what we'll do. I'll drive you there. I'll drive back. I'll visit Sugar. I'll drive back and pick you up. I'll drive you home. You'll be gone four hours. Tops, five, if there's traffic.

Traffic, she said.

There won't be any, I said. Not on a Saturday.

Several nights a week I walked through the park, around a weed-clogged pond to his house. I could see myself going there. I could watch myself from the corner and say, What is she doing? Stop. Don't go there. Sometimes I went to the front door, other times he met me in the garage. I won't talk about this even now except to say that years later when I was a different person living in a different place, the same intercom system was still on the house. I had gone back to kill him. I had a knife. It was unreasonable, ridiculous. My sister was in the car and she knew nothing. The knife was a cheap, pocket gadget that I had to use two hands to open. I had an idea I'd get him to let me in somehow. But a strange man's voice came through on the intercom. I asked for him and the stranger said he'd moved, didn't know where to. I saw no one. I heard only the voice over the intercom. I stood outside with my knife under my coat. I got back in the car with my sister.

The day arrived. A beautiful spring afternoon. The mansion manager showed me the dog and the collar and took me to the door and showed me the steps she walked out on to let the dog into the yard and the five minutes she waited in the kitchen and the words that she used to call the dog back and the pitch and the tone of it: Sugar! Sugar-baby! We did a few test runs. I examined the light switches, the locks, and the windows. I looked at the bathroom and the toilet paper, listened to instructions about the phone (not to answer). When there was at last nothing else to look at and no more to say, we put on our jackets and left the apartment.

Like anything or anyone, like two normal people, we drove off into the sunset — like the end of something or the beginning — or not quite, the sun wouldn't set for another hour.

It turned out I was in fact really sick in the head because I followed the plan exactly as we discussed. I dropped the manager off, then drove off with the sunset behind me, back to the Victorian mansion. Mansion is a big word for what it was. It didn't look that big from the front. There may be a strict line between what makes something a mansion or a house. A number of feet it must be over or under, a rule about whether grounds or porches count, a number of requisite rooms. If dogs had anything to do with it, the house was certainly covered in that department because there were seven deformed ones downstairs barking and one on the first floor for whom I was responsible. Who growled at me when I tried to take his collar like the manager showed me so that I had to kind of shoo him out into the yard with a rolled-up newspaper.

I waited in the kitchen and then went out to the steps and said, Sugar! Sugar-baby!

The dog did not come.

Sugar! Sugar-baby!

The dog was gone.

I walked down the steps. I walked a deep square around the yard, stopped at the back gate. Unlatched.

I looked everywhere. I ran down the alley through the shadows and then the slices of street of our neighborhood, the lights blinking on. I covered every foot that I could, saying, Sugar! Sugar-baby. I was panting. I rang the other bells in the house. I ran from front to back poking bushes.

I did it all and then I went back to get the manager. By now it was dark and I was driving sort of hysterically, swerving around on the road, and I got a little lost. For a moment I thought I'd lost the road completely and was on an entirely different road, one that would lead me somewhere entirely different, to some other person who needed to be picked up or dropped off, some other person yet to know they'd lost the one they loved, and then I would be in that story instead of this one. Or maybe the road would lead nowhere and I would be eternal, forever going, forever coming, like a mortal saved or punished by an ancient god. But it turned out I wasn't on that road, I was where I was supposed to be, everything was in its proper place, including her and the friend's house, heaping into view and there she was, the manager. She was waiting outside, huddled in the dark alone. I pulled up and she jumped in.

There isn't any other way to say this: She slammed the door like a car chase and said she'd been raped. She said it like an announcement or a prophecy or the denial or fulfillment of one.

Oh my God, I said. How.

There was a man in the bathroom. He grabbed my throat. I think he also wanted my purse.

Did he crawl in the window?

I believe he was a guest.

Did you call the police? I said. We better go to the police.

I have to get home.

Let's go to the police.

Take me home, she said.

She wouldn't talk about it, about the man in the bathroom. I tried again but she refused. There are things I too will never describe.

What happened in that bathroom? When I consider all the things in the world I don't know but one day will, these are not included. Another is not who punched out my front teeth a few days later. Several men were present. I don't know if it was the man I had and had not stopped seeing or if it was one of his friends. At the time of the event I could have asked and maybe they would have told me. But I was too disgraced to speak. I don't believe I would ask even now, given the chance. My shame is not a leaky bucket running out.

Later when I was living someplace else, it was months before I could even have a thought that wasn't spoken to him in my head. I would think about one sentence he had said for weeks at a time. Once for example I had told him I couldn't think of any reason to do one thing over the other.

I can, he said. There's the law.

I didn't know which law he was talking about, the Bible or the cops. Or if having a law was a reason to do something or not do something, if he meant to obey or trespass. Knowing him, it could go either way. I could have questioned him about it. I made lists in my head, for weeks I made lists of the things I could have asked: Do you mean absolute or relative law? Later the questions became accusations: I don't see you starting or stopping any revolutions! Later the words became slurred ones I woke with that I couldn't figure out.

We got back to the house and she opened the door to her apartment.

He's gone, she said. Where is my dog?

Look, even later the thing made no sense: The dog was in, the dog was out, the dog was gone.

Let's call the police, I said. We have so much to tell them.

What did you do with my dog? she screamed.

In the attic apartment there lived a man in an orange cap. That is all I can say about him. He went in and out. Later there was a disturbance involving the authorities and then he was gone. Soon I was gone, too. I told no one, dropped the key in the manager's mailbox, drove off in the dark with only what I could fit into my car. It didn't end there.

LUCK

ANGELA BALL

There was an Akita in Japan who went to the train every day to meet its master — even after the master died. At the station they put up a statue of the dog. The statue was melted down in WWII for gunmetal. After the war, they replaced it.

I have one of the small doors through which pets can come and go. Frank, a cat, slowly killed a bird for me last night.

When I was five, a dwarf pony was born. We named him John. The newspaper took a photo of the deformed foal, whose hooves met the ground at odd angles. Circus people came in a tall black car that looked about to fall over. They wanted to buy John. My older sister said we would never sell. The circus people got back

95.

into their car and drove away, sadly. A week later, John went missing.

The neighbor girl saw a fox balancing on a fence post and called for her father. She had seen the rabies movie. She wanted her father to shoot the fox, and he did. The fox's brain was sent to the state laboratory to be dissected. We all felt glad to be part of the scientific age.

LECTURE

REBECCA EVANHOE

We're still fighting all these people, even today.
All right. That's a cave. This is what he said.
And they're carrying implements! Nobody knows what these
implements are. But here, okay,
implements
and he gets the thing off the head and the shackles and
at first he thinks his face is burning off!
And he sees the bark and the people and the little dogs running
around . . .
This is the truth!
And he runs back — Take off your hats!
There is a big reality, there is this thing, and we sometimes we
can know it all, but it exists and it's out there!

perfect love perfect *cup*

Slowly, this has been crumbled. This is beginning to crumble. This is crumbling.

Descartes he was like the perfect person to try to resolve all this—science, and like, mathematics.

So then you had all these people coming in and hacking away at that.

Around 1890 the real trouble began.

I made slides well they don't have slides at this school, but I made these things.

So with WWI, these people were saying we're marching closer and closer to the truth—why aren't we marching closer and closer to goodness?

And then there was Freud, and people were more complex than *this is me I walk across the room.*

Everything is moving! Where's the one thing?

Our friend Alex.

A NOTE ABOUT THE STEPS TO
MR. POPPER'S OFFICE

CLANCY MARTIN

There were thirty-seven steps to Mr. Popper's office. At the top of the carpeted steps was the heavy closed door. The light was dim in the stairwell, the stairwell was narrow and high and there was no electrical outlet on the stairwell. Bill could vacuum to the twenty-ninth stair and then he had to move the cord. To move the cord he had to open the door to Mr. Popper's office. He was afraid to. But the only outlet that would reach the last eight stairs was in Mr. Popper's office. The carpet on the stairs was deep red with a vein of gold and emerald green. Bill vacuumed the stairs every morning before the store opened. He was on the stairs on his hands and knees when he felt a tap on his back. He looked up and saw Mr. Popper. Mr. Popper was short. He had a round, white face and a huge potbelly. He was wearing a pink Hermès tie. He always wore Hermès ties, which were purchased for him by his wife Sylvia, who was hated by everyone at the store, except for Bill's older brother Jim, because she had made Jim her protégé. The older salesmen at the store had tried to hate Jim as well but he was impossible to hate. "Good morning, Bill," Mr. Popper said. Bill smiled up at Mr. Popper and wondered if he should turn off the vacuum cleaner or keep vacuuming. It was a strong handheld Red Devil vacuum cleaner with a wide metal mouth and a red cloth bag. The cord was also wrapped in red and black cloth. Mr. Popper held his cowboy hat in his hand. "Good morning, Mr. Popper," he said. Mr. Popper gave him a look and Bill realized he was blocking the stairwell. So he turned off the vacuum cleaner and stood and pressed himself against the wall. He hoped Mr. Popper would say something about the stairs but Mr. Popper squeezed by him and continued up the stairs and opened the door and went into his office. Bill always finished vacuuming the stairs before Mr. Popper was in the store. He was pleased that now Mr. Popper knew who vacuumed his stairs every morning but he did not know what to do about the last eight stairs. He had never opened the door to Mr. Popper's office while Mr. Popper was in his office. But he could not finish the stairs without opening the door. If he knocked on the door Mr. Popper would think he wanted something. He only needed to finish the stairs, but Mr. Popper would think, who knew what. He would also be interrupting him. He might be on the phone. What if he was on the phone and he had to get up to answer the door, and there he was on the stairs, how would he explain that he needed to use the outlet in his office to finish the stairs? It was the sort of thing you could never explain. He could not just open the door with Mr. Popper in there. Jim told him the most important vacuuming was the vacuuming of Mr. Popper's stairs. "You don't think he notices, but he notices everything," Jim said. That was why Jim was on the floor as fast as he was, and now he was sales manager, and the best salesman in the store. But he had started vacuuming Mr. Popper's stairs. He thought about going to find an extension cord, but he didn't know where there was one, if there was one, and he didn't know who to ask, and the store would be opening any minute, and what would Mr. Popper think, hearing the vacuuming and then not hearing it, and then hearing it again a long time after it had stopped, and after the store was already open? And what if he came down to watch the store open, since he usually came in after the store was open, and he saw that the last eight steps were unvacuumed, while he was finding an extension cord, or if he came down after he found the cord, and he saw that he was still vacuuming, and thought it had taken him all that time to vacuum the stairs or, still worse, that the quiet minutes had been him sitting on the stairs, resting, not vacuuming or working at all, but hiding from work unseen at the top of the stairs, thinking he was so clever he could hide from work, while all the time Mr. Popper could hear that he hadn't been working at all, he had just been sitting there lazily on the stairs, when in fact he was trying to find an extension cord? But he couldn't knock on the door, and he couldn't open the door, and he couldn't try to find an extension cord, and he couldn't leave the last eight stairs unvacuumed.

THE BEST JEWELER

CLANCY MARTIN

Old John was a former helicopter gunner who held the first bench in my jewelry store. We had a strict system: the best jeweler sat up front, where he could watch the teenage girls go in and out of Victoria's Secret through the front window. Larry, our second-best bench man, sat behind Old John, and behind Larry Tommy, et cetera, down to the back of the store where the polishing wheels were. I kept a list of best to worse. The one exception was my wax carver Christian Hilburn, who always held the last bench because he claimed you couldn't carve waxes with people watching. Unlike many jewelry stores we kept the jewelers out where the customers could observe them. I knew my customers would worry about their jewelry less, while it was being worked on, if they could keep an eye on it. We always kept exactly seven guys on the bench.

Although Old John used solder to fill in the gaps in his channel setting he was a patient jeweler, and was the only one who could reliably work with platinum without costing me money. He never broke diamonds, not even the corners on princess cuts. He worked late like me. But I came in early and we never asked Old John to come in before noon. Often, after the store was closed and everyone else had gone home, he would tell me about his time as a gunner in Vietnam, or his year in prison in Mexico, or the seven years he did at Leavenworth, in Kansas, where he learned to be a jeweler. It's a fact many people don't know, that most jewelers and watchmakers learn how to sit on the bench while in prison.

He dyed his hair jet black. He kept a jade-handled forty-five chained to his bench. At Christmas he brought his boa in for the late nights and fed it mice in the store. He was five foot five. He drove a small, light, bruised Ford truck. His cheeks were as yellow and shiny as the belly of a lizard. His lunch and his dinner came to work with him in Tupperware, and he brought his own special coffee in a canteen. He did not drink or smoke, and unlike almost every other jeweler I have ever known, he didn't take speed or cocaine. I admired his asceticism. He kept the store square because he gave me a model to live by.

Good years Old John would make two hundred grand working for me, which is more than I ever paid myself. That didn't include the gold sweeps, colored stones and diamond melee that went home with all our jewelers at night in the pockets of their aprons. For years I had washed the aprons at night for the sweeps but two years ago I had stopped doing that, for personal reasons. Old John on the other hand was very good about that. He made a living and he did not want to cheat me. He never stole any sweeps or melee. He never did side work on company time, either.

Old John was the best jeweler in the Dallas-Fort Worth metroplex. I knew it and I was grateful for him. Everyone tried to steal him from me. But no one could. Those evening talks of ours made a difference, I believed. Normally I refused to make friends with employees but in Old John's case it was crucial. Then the woman came. Her name was Jane. You think, an ordinary name, but oh ho, look out. He did not tell me himself, of course, and you wouldn't have heard it around the shop because the other jewelers were afraid to tease him, but I finally got the word out of our shop manager Nathan. "John's got a girl," he said. We were sitting in my office talking about the new Plano store. It was losing twenty grand a month. I hoped to close it down. He was trying to convince me not to, and I worried why.

Old John lived with his mother and had never dated anyone as far as we knew, so this was alarming news. I had supposed on the way home he usually stopped at Rosie's Gentleman Tan. "What?" I said. "She's a new saleswoman over at Victoria's Secret. John's been watching her for weeks. Now he's started coming in before nine to watch her on her way in." I came in at seven, turned off the alarms and opened the safes, and then worked in my office until it was time to put out the cases, so I had not noticed. Nathan was grinning. He stroked his nose with his index finger. He had nice fingers and a long nose. "Has he spoken to her?" I asked him.

I was not grinning. I understood Nathan was warning me. He often did that, perhaps without realizing it. "No," Nathan said. "But I'm going to go and give her a coupon for a free tighten and polish and invite her in. She wears a lot of jewelry." "Jewelry?" I was surprised. Some people should own jewelry and others should not. "No, cheap stuff," he said. "You know, titty-dancer jewelry." I said firmly, "Be certain to tell me when she comes in." I knew she would be in. I made Nathan shop manager not because he knew the business — he couldn't do much more than stretch rings and polish — but because he could sell and his look. I can tell you now, that is the secret to a successful shop: have a manager who can sell the job. That was our trouble up in Plano. Lisa couldn't sell. She knew jewelry. She was a GIA-certified gemologist. But she looked like hell. It frustrated and confused me that I had made her a manager.

Nathan went to work on Jane like he could when he wanted to and before you knew it Jane and Old John were going to lunch three times a week. Jane looked exactly like the young woman you picture when you picture the young woman who works at Victoria's Secret. She called him John, which we all did, but she could call him John to his face. That made me angry. She would ring on the phone in the afternoon and say, "May I speak to John, please?" True, she said please. Old John only received phone calls once or twice a month and then it was his mother. He took Jane's calls in the same place he took his mother's: in the back bathroom, with the door closed, and the phone cord stretched all the way under the door. The cord wasn't that long and you wondered if he had to lie on the bathroom floor to get the phone up against his ear. He was so clean I doubted it. His fingernails were like clear epoxy. You do not see that in jewelers. Down on the floor in the piss. We had our own bathroom on our side. But this was the jeweler's bathroom.

I could manage Old John's affair but then Jane decided to come to the regular showroom, our showroom, and befriend my salespeople. Normally the Victoria's Secret girls knew better than to come in our place. They were modest enough. There was no point coming in if you couldn't spend a thousand bucks. We didn't have anything for less than a grand, not even in the watchcases. We didn't waste time with porcelain figurines and crystal vases. We were a luxury jewelry store.

The problem was obvious. This woman Jane hung around in Martin's, flirted with Jim and Clancy, and then bounced over to waggle her tits at Old John and the boys on the bench. It was worse than untidy. She was taking over. I admit it was my fault because initially I was too busy to consider her. We were in trouble at the bank with an old line of credit and one of our investors was unforeseeably closing out a buy line he had funded that I had expected to use to pay back the bank. But the saleswomen were in and out of my office all day complaining about her. Especially Janice, who was trying to steal Clancy away from his wife and did not appreciate Jane's interference.

"She doesn't buy anything," Janice said. "If she bought something it would be different. She's not even a customer." She was standing by the door of my office cleaning her left ear with a pair of thirty-two dollar titanium-tipped diamond tweezers. "You know you shouldn't stick those in your ears, Janice," I told her. She looked at the tweezers. "Sorry," she said. She wiped them clean with a diamond cloth an appointment had left on my desk. That's why you put things away, Baron, I thought. "That's disgusting. I'm sorry. I do it without even knowing I'm doing it." "No," I said. I had the same problem. There was something in the air of the store that made your ears itchy. I think it was particles of red and yellow rouge from the polishing wheels. "But you could lose an ear drum." I hoped she would go away. Please go away, Janice, I thought. Then I thought, Baron, what kind of a boss are you? Suddenly I had no control over my people or my environment. It was as though the walls of my office momentarily fell down around us and my chair turned upside down. I was sick to my stomach. But she went on. "She just stands around all the time. I can't sell with her standing around like that. She acts like she works here. She doesn't work here." I wanted to ask her: Janice, when was the last time you put a number up on the boards? Things settled back into place. But the goal was for Janice to leave. Then if necessary I could put away Jane. "I'll talk to Old John about it," I said. "Sure you will," Janice said and made that face of hers that kept anyone from honestly trusting her. That face is why you cannot even sell a lousy TAG Heuer, Janice, I wanted to say. But at least she walked and I could get back to work.

I figured these things never solve themselves. The sooner I interfered the better. Then again, she might get bored of the attention and go back to Victoria's Secret where she fit in well.

But I also acknowledged that my argument, though valid, was not sound, because one premise was false. Titty dancers do not grow bored of attention. Not that Jane was a titty dancer in the strict sense so far as I knew. Truly I'd never known a titty dancer. I don't even use the expression. But she was a kind of socioeconomic equivalent.

Many jewelers I have employed show an angry face at the bench. The metal is their enemy. That's one way of doing it. But Old John wore a precise, cunning smile while he worked. He was holding a secret. So when I saw Old John Friday afternoon setting my three-carat padparadscha sapphire with his lips folded together like a pair of scissors I knew I had a problem I could no longer afford to tolerate. On the one hand I wasn't worried about the sapphire, corundum is tough, it was an oval so no corners, and it was one of my new twenty-two carat designs, a Late-Byzantine Elizabeth Gage knock-off, so the metal was as soft as frozen butter. I knew Old John wouldn't let even Jane affect his work at the bench. On the other hand it makes me mad but most times you lose good people you lose them for personal reasons, so I called Nathan into my office.

"Nathan," I questioned him, "fine, you were right. You knew and I didn't. So now tell me what I need. What must I do about Jane?" Nathan squirmed. He played with something in his lap. I thought: No. No warning. Of course. Not Nathan. "I didn't mean to," Nathan said. His head wandered childishly. "She licked my neck," he apologized.

Thousands of people every year fall in love in jewelry stores.

My employees were constantly fucking each other. Dating policies were useless. They even fell in love with customers. Customers! It is because of the diamonds and platinum, the rubies and gold. You should not mix them. That is why the great jewelry cultures—Thailand, India, Israel—are all grossly oversexed. Think about Canadians. They hate jewelry. But who has ever fucked a Canadian?

So now because of my slovenliness and Jane too it was Nathan or Old John. This was of course an inadmissible disjunction. The next day Jim was late for work and when he called in I already knew so, resigned, I told Julie to put him through to my office. I checked my Patek. It was nearly eleven-thirty. I noticed through the one-way glass that the Anteater, the Gypsy, was snooping around the antique case. I hoped all the cases were locked. Clancy was not on the floor. The Anteater waved at a piece and I watched Janice turn and run for the back. The soles of my feet were sweating and I kicked off my wingtips. I picked up the phone.

"You're not going to believe this, boss," Jim whispered over the line. He always called me boss because he thought it kept him on my good side. It was true from him I enjoyed it. "You're at Jane's," I said. "What? How did you know?" he said. I could tell he was smiling on the other end. That was why Jim was one hell of a salesman, my second-best, because he was joyful like a little boy. He was cute, too, he was the kind of guy you would sleep with and in the morning he would tell you he loved you and then he would be mystified and insulted when you laughed. He was sincere. Like a boy or an angel. No brains though.

"Take the day off," I told him. I saw my opportunity now. "Keep her out of the store. Keep her out of Arlington if you can. I have to figure this out." I thought I understood what to do. Then I wondered if I was merely panicking. I suffered a vision of Jane fucking Jim. She was on top. I called Nathan. He picked up the phone and asked me, "Have you heard from Old John?" Christian asked me. I could hear sloppy polishing in the background. The wheels were shrieking. Larry. Probably drunk. That kind of metalwork cost me ten cents a second. "What?" At this point I did not precisely want to shoot myself but I wanted to shoot someone else. "He left early yesterday and he hasn't called." I thought, What about my two-carat bezel-set studs? Stan Bowler had an appointment at one. That was twenty-three grand I had to have in the bank at opening Monday morning or my checks to Davidoff, IDC, Simons, all of them would bounce. "I put Christian on the platinum studs," Nathan said. "He's hobnailing them now. I checked." Good Nathan, I thought. "But his pistol's gone too," Nathan said. "Okay," I said. "Remind Christian the studs are screw backs," I said and hung up the phone. Then I found Clancy, put him in charge, and drove to Old John's.

I knew to go to Old John's because once before, years ago when we were all at Fort Worth Gold together, Old John had taken a customer hostage in the mailroom. It was a confusion over a ring. The customer claimed that Old John had switched stones on him. He was wrong, of course, but that was not the point. The point was that Old John fell into a Vietnam regression or who knew what and took the customer hostage, tied him to a chair with copper alloy wire and kept him there in the mailroom with the barrel of this same missing jade-handled pistol stuck in the customer's mouth. No one knew what to do: it was Old John, after all. We weren't going to call the police. But Ronnie Popper, who was the owner of Fort Worth Gold and Silver Exchange, and who was a kind of uncanny salesman-avatar who could close a deal just by gesturing, like a magician, without even speaking to the customer, intuited that we needed Old John's mother. I was seventeen years old and the head runner then. I did everything but the bank deposits, so I was sent to get her. She was calm and gentle. When we arrived at the store she walked into the mailroom without speaking to him or anyone else, took the gun away from Old John, put it in her red leather purse, and packed them both into the car. Old John and herself, I mean, the customer was still tied up. They sat there and waited for me to drive them home. I was eager to hear the conversation from the back seat but they sat silently together the whole way. She only spoke once, to ask me to pull into a McDonald's and get them Filet-O-Fish sandwiches. Later I heard Mr. Popper gave the customer a Rolex so he wouldn't press charges. Mr. Popper was that kind of a boss. When I sold my first Men's President, before I was even on the sales floor, he had hugged me and tucked a hundred dollar bill into my shirt pocket.

With Jane, Old John and Jim I held a similar situation in my hands. Hopefully it wouldn't be necessary to give away any Rolexes. We weren't making the kind of money Popper used to. But when I got to Old John's mom's place the cops were already there.

Two prowlers were parked in the driveway with their lights spinning. I hung my jacket in the car, then thought twice and folded it in the passenger seat, and approached. The door was open. It was my job to go in. From upstairs in the house I could hear people laughing. This was disorienting. It should be encouraging, I thought. I was abruptly unsure whether or not I should involve myself so I wandered back to where I imagined the kitchen must be to wash my hands. And there at the kitchen table was Old John's mother with Jane, a policeman and another old woman I didn't know. They were drinking coffee and picking at a vegetable tray. Old John's mother stood carefully and I saw she was bent like a violin from osteoporosis but otherwise unchanged. She said, "Baron dear! See how you've grown!" I must have looked frightened because she said, "Don't worry." Then she asked me, "Do you know John's friend Jane?" "Hi Jane," I said. Jane winked at me. She was wearing a white tank top with a round pink bird on one breast. The cop introduced himself, he had a Coke in his hand, and I met Pearl, who was Old John's mom's sister. Unlike her sister, Pearl stood perfectly straight. "Where's Old John?" I asked. "Old John?" his mother asked. "He's upstairs with Jim," Jane said.

"Nathan's here too, Baron," Old John's mom said.

Without realizing what I was doing I sat down in Old John's mom's chair. The cop gave me a look and then rose and fetched a chair out of the dining room for Old John's mom. "I'm sorry," I said. Old John's mom said, "Never mind, honey," and sat back down. She passed me a cup. "Would you like some coffee, Baron?"

I didn't know what to ask next. Jane abruptly laughed. I wanted to explain that I was only trying to help. Then I wanted to ask everyone to get back to work. "I think I need to get back to the store," I said. "We are in trouble at the bank." "Everything is going to be all right, Baron," Old John's mom said and took my hand in hers. Her palm was wet. I thought, these people are living lives I cannot conceive. I looked at the four of them and they smiled generously back at me. They tried to draw me out into a circle of their laughter. I realized I would never enjoy an explanation.

PAPER

FORREST ROTH

I wrote many, many letters to Mrs. Sawana. They were all about the same in content and expression: *I belong to you*, or *It's something I said, isn't it?* In lieu of my signature at the bottom of the page was the orange dot made by the tip of my nose. My anonymity to all — besides Mrs. Sawana — was assured. The stationery paper I used was common, untraceable, as was hers.

Write to me. Tell me who you are, she wrote in furtive strokes.

I had been following advice for men in a magazine I used to read. Thinking the gesture romantic (and, I vaguely hoped, erotic), I sprayed some of my favorite cologne at the end so she might recognize me later. When I was done smelling the page, I realized I had left a small impression of sweat where my signature would normally be. It dried into a dirty brown film. I took my business ink pad, pressed the tip of my nose into it, and covered the offending mark. The best work of all lovers is created through the concealment of accidents, I reflected.

Hana no in'kan: a nose intaglio. Orange ink, sebaceous. Elliptical circle. Tiny dots, the pores raised off the paper's surface. A signet? That was not my name being sent to her, nor even my pseudonym should her husband stumble upon her carelessness. That was the point where she started.

"My little orange dot," she whispered, directing her kiss to the edge of that piece of cartilage I took for granted. No feeling came from it. It could not blush on its own, so I did to compensate. I glowed, frightened and ticklish.

She had no such center of gravity. I almost didn't know what to do. Her body seemed uniform; each proceeding part responded the same to me as the previous one. Flush of movement followed the course of her blood and mine. She nearly flung herself out of my arms. Then she finally welcomed the rest of my body. The sun rose and set beneath her as she did so.

My little orange dot, she began, *we should have met sooner.*

I gave up wearing cologne once I learned what she adored. A childish joke we shared — yet painful in its simple truth — soon materialized: I brought a single flower to her each time, knowing it would have to be discarded that same day before she returned home.

Mrs. Sawana, I wrote, *I hope to give you a flower that you will keep.*

A joke always becomes serious when repeated often. I considered whether to use better paper to write to her, with enmeshed flora. Etsuko offered to make a personal sheet for me. "What does she like?" she asked. Camelia, azelia, hydrangea. Blades of short grass under her feet, too, freshly cut. She had just the right mixture in mind, the appropriate texture for obedient fingers. "This sounds serious," she unfortunately added. Upon further consideration, I told her to wait.

The correspondence remained prolific and lively. My desk filled with letters, all of which were addressed to my favored olfactory peak. I remained confident that I was somewhere behind her words. When we met, I felt certain my identity was saved in her caresses.

The mark became the source of my pride. Every pressing carefully deliberated. After I sent the letters I often forgot what I wrote.

She eventually did not respond to each letter.

My little orange dot, she replied, *is getting bigger. Are you pressing too hard?*

This particular letter concerned me.

I walked to and from the train station with my head down. I worried that the tip of my nose, perhaps becoming stained permanently from the ink, would give me away. I washed it with determination and looked at it closely in the mirror for diamonds buried underneath its surface. I buffed it with cheesecloth and cooled it with ice cubes. I took it for walks at night and let it lead me to her doorstep brazenly as she slept with her husband. I stuffed it with tiny balls of tissue so it could keep shape. I had the priest bless it at my local temple, who could not perform the service without a concerned smile. There are no sutras for the deliverance of inflamed nasal passages, he explained. We burned incense anyway.

Mrs. Sawana, I wrote, *you are being served well, but not by me.*

I wasn't certain what I was waiting for, if not her.

I patted the space on the stone bench where she would have sat next to me.

The day grew late. She surprised me by kissing my lips first and only. Besides one more letter, nothing else followed.

It is over, my little orange dot, she wrote. *Take care of yourself, and that which I loved the most.*

I asked Etsuko to make the paper I had originally wanted, though she told me not to brood over the whole affair. I promised her I wouldn't. She took my hand for a moment. I said nothing. She left me feeling slightly guilty.

The paper arrived in the mail with prompt courtesy. About two dozen cut pages. It was bundled with a crepe sash that carried an invocation for the writer, which is the custom here among the paper-makers: *Respect the pen, honor this paper, revere those addressed.*

Obeying the invocation, I waited for several days.

Mrs. Sawana, I began, *will I have a name someday?*

CHINESE APPLES

FORREST ROTH

Mother still calls pomegranates "Chinese apples," much to my embarrassment. A bowl filled with them sits on our den table. "Look at this, a Chinese apple!" she will say, as if it suddenly dropped from a perfumed cloud, while our guest remains silent. She's an expert at presentation: taking a paring knife, she cuts the fruit at its equator and, breaking it open, produces two perfect halves. Not a single seed falls. She lets our guest look upon the juicy bouquet; he has yet to say whether he actually wants any or not. Curious of the offer, he reaches in to try one, searching her face for the appropriate response he should take. "Eat," she commands, "and don't worry about the floor." He listens to her, and while they spit seeds on the carpet, I try to explain — will it never end? — that pomegranates didn't come from China originally, but Persia. "Well," she says in between seeds, "it's only a name I enjoy, dear." Spit spit spit.

NATURE

FORREST ROTH

She arrived unsure about being here. I put her at her ease during dinner. The candles, she said; it was the only difference she needed, but I wanted her to see more.

I took her out back to view the statue up close. She didn't seem impressed. We walked down to the dock. She was bored completely. I showed her the old stone well not far away. She wanted to die.

Throw yourself in, I told her.

He felt the disappointing pause.

So that's all that happened to her?

I'LL BE AVAILABLE WHILE TRAVELING

YASMINE ALWAN

My grandfather, a Turk, had had the choice of leaving, among other privileges. I never met him. In pictures he grips the arms of his chair as if he is about to be tipped out, his neck stretched. Well, he says, his face remote after a silence, this is what it must be like for someone like me to meet someone like you.

Because I always move west on this street, I cross traffic toward the Middle Eastern places. I put a tissue into my pocket, even though I don't need one. I walk around with it in my pocket all day, half sticking out. I think about it there throughout the afternoon. I can feel it, while I drink my wine and push my toe in the sunny gravel, in the way that you can feel money in your wallet.

I had started out working at a Popsicle plant in Ronkonkoma,

New York. I individually wrapped Popsicles, sealing each with a heat clamp. The wrappers were cut from an infinite see-through plastic sleeve, unspun from a giant spool.

In English my grandmother used to tell me, Go jump in a lake. In Arabic she'd curse me, Stick a screwdriver up your ass. She is there also, sitting in the longer poolside chairs, the ones that you can lie entirely out on, feet up, with short tin schnauzer legs that make a discomforting scraping sound on the cement when you get up. She has a sheer scarf over her hair, her sneakers on like she used to in the young days, and all her skin is rubbed down with Vaseline, so that she is in a constant state of absorption. She tries to rub the pretty marks off my face with an oily thumb.

PARTIAL LIST OF
PEOPLE TO BLEACH

GARY LUTZ

She was either next to me on a plane and turning a page of her magazine every time I turned a page of mine, or else she had come forward from way back to be a handful anew, because people repeat on you or otherwise go unplundered. I'll think of her as Aisler for any priggish intentions I might still manage here.

Aisler had spousy eyes, and arms exemplary in their plunges, and she brought her bare knees together until they were buttocky and personal. But I hemmed and hawed inside of her and never got the hang of her requirements. A woman that swaggering of heart will not bask in deferred venereal folderol.

Anyway, she had a kid, and the kid's questions kept tripping me up—e.g., if you let people walk all over you, do you become a place? This kid: there already were tiny whelms of hair all over him.

Some beds are on wheels, but see how far it'll get you.

The day after they left, I made a study of the lease. I'd never given much thought to its terms before. There was a lessor, and a lessee. From either end, this looked like uncomplicating deduction, subtraction. In short, I left the apartment the way I had found it — evacuated, incapacitated for any glorying course of residential circumstance.

I was not right in the heart, or wrong about much else.

At the office campus, there was a new hire on my level. She looked boxed up in her compact, median twenties: unpackable. It was all I could do to show her the quickest way to disable a paper clip so it could no longer get a purchase on the pages, how to refuse food from people who came in one day with new teeth shingled over the old. But there was no concord to come, no rumoring of prim bedtime enterprise. My other associates sank further in lacklustrous matrimonies, carried on without bywords or forays. I'd skim some minutes off an arriving hour for some jaunty pleasance in the john. Aside from that, I never gleamed in my attendance.

In theory, then, there were the taken, and the takers, and, between them, people like me, local to the outside world.

Until it turned out my new workmate had a brother, a stifler, but precise in his shrugs, his fingerworthy allure. I was a stopgap pursuit of his for an afternoon of unbegged-for undress.

I let him refer the bleaky broth of his semen into me.

I felt bumped up in his affections even as his hand was already deadening on my knee.

(This was in a duplex shy of shelving, of furnitures.)

But there was actually a third sibling, he was afterward claiming — someone closer to my own, lavish age, and catastrophized more quietly. Adrowse undrunkenly in a bathtub upstairs. The water hued and perfumed and kept constantly bubblish, thanks to a pump, should I want to risk a famishing look.

But a day gets mussed from stunts some hearts kept attempting.

It widens as you tire of it.

This still was Thursday. Then Friday finally underfoot. Then a three-day weekend, a second-string holiday it was necessary to observe.

I knew enough to go home, to my folks.

My parents — they had each overshot their marriage but otherwise went about ungulfed by life. They welcomed me back to their shams. Nothing was amiss or cosmic in my old, dormered room upstairs. A promising first gush of sleep, and then I awoke to the usual voices pluming upward through the baseboards.

Mother, Father: these two mingled mostly in my destructions, took their customary tack in my backpedaling.

Friends of theirs at length tipped me off to a splashy woman who claimed you can always tell when one is going to go on to ape something wonderful or when he should have all along been hoping to be better known as more of a mama's boy.

Sometimes people get too close to call.

CONTRIBUTORS

Yasmine Alwan lives in New York and received her MFA from Bard College's Milton Avery Graduate Program of the Arts in 2005.

Angela Ball teaches in the Center for Writers at the University of Southern Mississippi in Hattiesburg.

Kim Chinquee's work has recently appeared in *NOON*, *Cottonwood*, *Conjunctions*, *Denver Quarterly*, *elimae*, and other journals.

Rebecca Curtis is an Assistant Professor of English at the University of Kansas. Her fiction has appeared in *Harper's*, *The New Yorker*, and elsewhere, and is forthcoming in *McSweeney's* and *Harper's Bazaar Australia*. She lives in Brooklyn.

Lydia Davis is the author, most recently, of *Samuel Johnson Is Indignant* (McSweeney's, 2001) and the translator of the new *Swann's Way* by Marcel Proust (Viking Penguin, 2003), which was awarded the French-American Foundation Prize for Translation.

Rebecca Evanhoe's "Lecture" is her first published story. She lives in Lawrence, Kansas.

Augusta Gross is a frequent contributor to *NOON*. She is a psychologist who formerly practiced in New York City. She is also a pianist and composer.

Bill Hayward is a photographer who lives and works in New York City. The photographs featured are from Hayward's *The American Memory Project*—a forthcoming series of books, films, and traveling exhibitions. This project can be followed at theamericanmemoryproject.com

Gary Lutz is the author of *Stories in the Worst Way* and *I Looked Alive*.

Clancy Martin has published stories, poems, and essays in *NOON*, *Parakeet*, *Philosophy and Literature*, and *Analecta*, among others. His new translation of Nietzsche's *Thus Spoke Zarathustra* is forthcoming from Barnes and Nobles Classics. He lives in Lawrence, Kansas.

Neal Rantoul is head of the photography program at Northeastern University in Boston. His work is in numerous public and private collections including the Museum of Fine Arts, Boston, the High Museum of Art in Atlanta, the Kunsthaus Zürich, the Center for Creative Photography in Tucson, and the Fogg Art Museum at Harvard University. His book, *American Series*, is forthcoming from Pond Press in spring 2006. His work may be viewed at NealRantoul.com

Forrest Roth's fiction appears or is forthcoming in *Snow Monkey*, *Paragraph*, *elimae*, and other journals. He has completed a novel. He lives in Buffalo, New York.

Christine Schutt is the author of two collections of short stories, *Nightwork*, and the recently published, *A Day, a Night, Another Day, Summer*. Her first novel *Florida* was a finalist for the National Book Award, 2004.

Deb Olin Unferth's fiction has appeared in *Harper's*, *Conjunctions*, *NOON*, *Fence*, *3rd bed*, *StoryQuarterly*, *Denver Quarterly*, and other publications. She is the recipient of a Pushcart Prize and coeditor of the literary annual *Parakeet*. She lives in Lawerence, Kansas.

Rob Walsh's stories have appeared in *Redivider* and are forthcoming in *Fugue*. He lives in Seoul.

THE EDITORS WISH TO THANK THE FOLLOWING
INDIVIDUALS FOR THEIR GENEROUS SUPPORT OF NOON:

Anonymous

Katie Baldwin

The Balsamo Family Foundation

Margaret Barrett

Francis and Prudence Beidler

Lisa Bornstein

Melinda Davis and Ealan Wingate

Lawrie and Tony Dean

Joseph Glossberg

Ellen Kern

Christina Kirk

Laura S. Kirk

Lucy and Kenneth Lehman

Ruth and Irving Malin

Clancy Martin

Thea and David Obstler

Lily Tuck

Abby S. Weintraub

Paul C. Williams

A NOTE ON THE TYPE

This book was set in Fournier, a typeface named for Pierre Simon
Fournier, a celebrated type designer in eighteenth-century France.
Fournier's type is considered transitional in that it drew its inspira-
tion from the old style yet was ingeniously innovative, providing
for an elegant yet legible appearance. For some time after his death
in 1768, Fournier was remembered primarily as the author of a
famous manual of typography and as a pioneer of the print system.
However, in 1925 his reputation was enhanced when the Monotype
Corporation of London revived Fournier's roman and italic.

Typeset by Matt Mayerchak, Needham, Massachusetts
Printed and bound in Iceland by Oddi Printing
Cover design by Susan Carroll

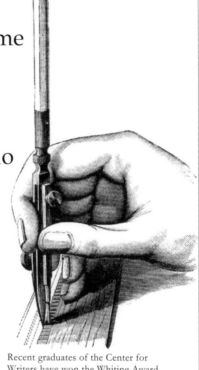

Permanent Faculty

Angela Ball
Frederick Barthelme
Julia Johnson
Steven Barthelme

Visiting Writers 2004-06

Lucie Brock-Broido
Stephen Dobyns
Percival Everett
James Kimbrell
Tim O'Brien
Francine Prose
Elissa Schappell
Matthew Sharpe
Julie Sheehan
Rob Spillman
James Tate
Dara Weir
Diane Williams

Recent graduates of the Center for Writers have won the Whiting Award, the Transatlantic Award, the *Playboy* Fiction Contest, and the Flannery O'Connor Award. Seven graduates published books with major publishers last year. Another couple are publishing books this year. We edit the *Mississippi Review* online and in paper, publish a student magazine, and manage, with a little luck, to help our writers become better writers. For information, please contact rief@mississippireview.com, call us at (601) 266-5600, or write us in that old-fashioned way.

THE CENTER FOR WRITERS

THE UNIVERSITY OF SOUTHERN MISSISSIPPI
118 COLLEGE DRIVE # 5144, HATTIESBURG, MS 39406-0001 AA/EOE/ADAI
WWW.CENTERFORWRITERS.COM

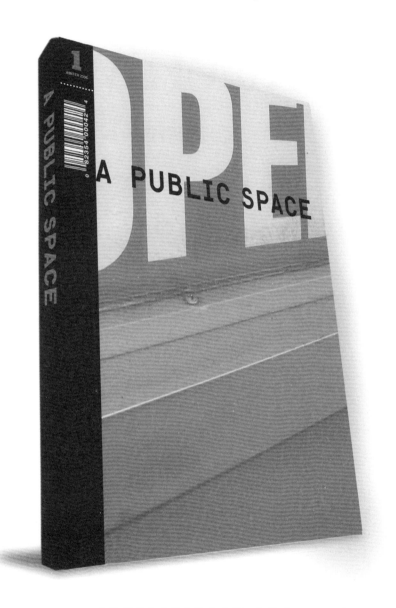

the PARIS REVIEW

DISCOVER

a new editor
PHILIP GOUREVITCH

a powerful mix

a captivating redesign

REDISCOVER

the essential
EXCELLENCE

the definitive interviews

the wit and the edge

SUBSCRIBE

"The Biggest
'Little' Magazine
in History"
—*Time*

KR

Provocative

Nervy

Influential

Essential.

The
Kenyon Review

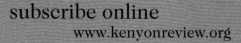

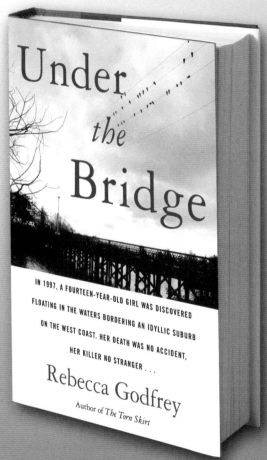

The National Book Award Finalist
New in Paperback

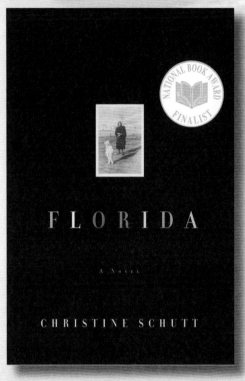

"Christine Schutt conveys real truths about childhood and longing.
She is truly a gifted writer."
—George Sauders, author of *Pastoralia*

"Beautiful and mean and elegantly wry . . . the story of storytelling—
and how it develops as a means to order one's disordered world."
—*The Believer*

"The luxury of this debut novel is its rich, descriptive language.
It's harnessed with powerful simplicity."
—*The Christian Science Monitor*

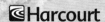 Harcourt
www.HarcourtBooks.com

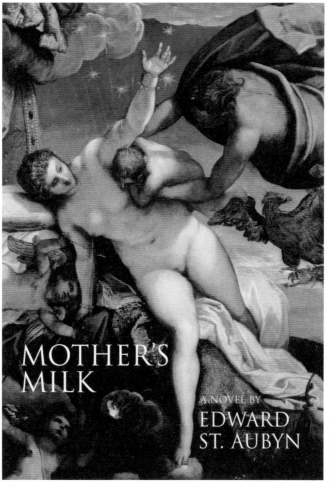

A *good* LUNCH

ONE HOT DISH
meat   *vegetables*

SANDWICH

FRUIT

✓ **WEST BRANCH**

WPA *SCHOOL* LUNCH

Poetry.Fiction.Essays.Reviews
Bucknell Hall, Bucknell University, Lewisburg, PA 17837
www.bucknell.edu/westbranch